Emergency Dream

In memory of Alice Wong, and for all disabled oracles, past, present and future.

Emergency Dream

Polly Atkin

SEREN BOOKS

Seren Books is the book imprint of
Poetry Wales Press Ltd.
Suite 6, 4 Derwen Road, Bridgend,
Wales, CF31 1LH

www.serenbooks.com
Follow us on social media @SerenBooks

ISBN: 978-1-78172-795-9

A CIP record for this title is available from the British Library.

The publisher acknowledges the financial assistance of the Books Council of Wales.

EU GPSR Authorised Representative
Logos Europe, 9 rue Nicolas Poussin, 17000,
La Rochelle, France
E-mail: Contact@logoseurope.eu

Cover artwork: 'Heart of the Forest, 1935' by Emily Carr.

Printed in Bembo by CMP.

'We tell our stories and truths in our own words. We define who we are and our place in the world. We fight to be seen and heard. We live in defiance with joy and radical acceptance. [...]

As disabled oracles, we continue to build and create on the knowledge and dreams of our ancestors. They left their mark on the planet as will we. After we're long gone, we will show up in other ways. Someone will see and discover us and we'll be speaking with them from the past.'

– *Alice Wong*

'By the time the apocalypse began, the world had already
ended. It ended every day for a century or two. It ended, and another ending world spun in its place.'

– *Franny Choi*

Contents

Season 1

Dislocation

'the Kingdom of the Sick is no democracy'
– *Sinéad Gleeson*

I have never been there, the country they call
Health. I used to believe I lived there,

was born there, citizen amongst citizens, inhabitant
of a familiar familial land, certain

when I moved in a crowd the crowd and I
stirred the same air with comparable bodies,

flattened the same ground, touched the same earth
in the same rain, under the same moon, in communion

and unity. But I have never been there,
not seen it, not even from a distance, the hazy

idea of it, a far shore gleaming from the wrong
side of an inland sea I could swim

to reach it, never stepped out into it, dissolved
in its throng, resident amongst residents, one

of them, never walked through the town with them, gone with them
into their clean, dry houses, never slept

the timeless sleep of the entirely comfortable,
never visited even for a day, never walked

its avenues, shaded by the leaves of its trees
rippling gently in a breeze I have never felt

on my skin, never softened at the press of its sun
like a hand on the nape of my neck, not even

in a dream, never dreamed I stared up at the sky
and said *these are the constellations of Health*

and knew them to navigate by them. I
was somewhere else all that time, something

else. Shadow in a shadow kingdom.
The blue light of Health cast me into long dark.

My bones my home, a republic out
of joint, always slipping from its sockets like I slip

between surfaces, the way I click back into
myself, belonging where I always belonged.

Pain Metaphors

It was sort of like a log smouldering on the fire.
It was all cracked black surface ash edges and ember.
It was glowing in its heart, but not in a joyful way, not
in a loving way. It was glowing with the tension of carbon
that wanted to be released. It was glowing with the lack
of attention you gave it. It was glowing with desperation

and your feet were two logs still smouldering, when you need
to put on another to keep the fire burning. Not close
enough to keep each other alight. You need to get up
get up on the pain and move them towards each other.
You need to use the poker. When you try to get up
they singe the rug, they singe the carpet. Each step sears.

An acrid smoke follows you like a dog at your heel,
your smouldering heel. You can't fit your shoes on
so you go out barefoot, logfoot – tap tap –
so every ground you walk on is a stage
trip trap trip trap or a troll bridge. You meet
your neighbours and they ask how you are and you say

not bad not bad except for my feet!
You gesture down at them, smoke hissing up
from the wet ground so thick you almost believe them
when they say they can't see what you mean but by then
it's crumbling like pillars of soot and it's everywhere –
in your hair, in your eyes, drawn into your lungs –

your blood is dust. You are washed down the road
in the rain and even that hurts and it

is a javelin skewered through your ribs and it
is your rib cage as fist, crushing your heart
and the three swords piercing it and it is the axe
lodged at the base of your skull since that dream
you had at fifteen, when you lost your head
in a derelict warehouse and died. It reminds you

you woke up and it is life. Rupturing.
Clamorous. Daily and far beyond time.
It is multitudes. It does not translate. It will not stop
speaking itself into flame.

Swim Craft

Hands forward palms together
like a prayer. You are good at mimicry – this
is how you learn – bad at discerning
the ways in which you differ. Hands
forward palms together like an arrow –
like your body is an arrow pointing towards
a shore you will not reach – a prayer
for movement with minimal disturbance. Now turn
your palms and part the world. You are cutting
the lake into wavering ribbons. You are folding
reflections. Layering fell and sky,
remixing them into each other in new
arrangements that rotate in your wake. Kick
them free. Let them evolve. You are
a spear, a knife, a mirror. You are cutting
a path that you cannot walk. You are turning
the device of the globe with your gliding. Kaleidoscope
swimmer, transfixed by the opening and closing
of the mountain within the water, the opening
of the mountain to let the sky dive through
the rock in synchronised blocks. Lost
in how they do it, agree on the order
in which to blend with each other, who rises
who falls. Always reforming. Swimmer,
don't forget yourself. You are the silent
mechanism inventing pattern as you draw
amazement out of colour.

Pain Metaphors

Disheartening is when your heart slips out of its dock
in the harbour of your ribs, falls through your chest
slides past your liver your kidneys your pelvis
and out and down, down through the floor
through the ground through the earth's crusty mantle and the walls
of your torso echo with its absence its negative
space. Disheartening is when a word or phrase
forms a long metal hook and enters your skull
through your eyeholes or ears extends down your gullet
and catches your heart, pulls it back up
and out through it. This is disheartening. When you feel
its chambers cave in, crushed from without,
when you feel it flatten all of a sudden,
all your blood fountaining out and you know
something has left you forever. This
is disheartening. When you can't get it back.

Flying in Dreams

Nine years old on the bottom step
down to the playground
where the tarmacs switch.

I've cherry blossoms hooked on my fingers
in pairs, like cherries. I'll keep them together
in my desk till there's no petals left.

This moment is fateful. I am stood on the steps
and nothing has changed except I've gained
this image – my five-year-old body in the sky.

I must try harder. If I run faster,
recover the correct articulation of limbs,
I could rise, keep rising, stay up forever.

Our mouths are gills for sky-fish. We lumber
around, grounded by collective forgetting.
Only in sleep do we know what we are.

When we dream we are flying
we are really swimming
through the thin water of the air.

Rural Architecture/Plague Year Season 1

Because the hotelier who bought the farm
started to knock down the barns that first
dry spring of the plague, just as the swallows
flew in to find a pyre in the yard –
old beams and asbestos smouldering darkly
like a public information film on apocalypse –
and turned on the wing – wouldn't you? – it's harder
each year to tell if the world is still working.
Swifts scream loops and circuits like fighter-jets
practising war overhead and you can't
hear your own thoughts for the martins chittering

but because the hotelier emailed to tell you
he always acts with respect for ecology
and heritage you wonder *working for whom?*
whose earth? what common ground? and because

he swore he'd never witnessed swallows
on his property, only a pair in the skies

you're grieving for air. In September you find
the tawny owl that haunted the barn
he took the roof off dead on the grass
by the main road, glanced by a car in the night,
and feel something fall in the woods, as though
a huge tree was axed at the root, centuries
of dwelling hewn to lumber. There's a mechanism
gone and an off-beat ticking. The swallows
will return, but not to the farm.

Burying the Owl

You buried everything you have ever known
and could ever learn in the raised bed
by the front door of your rented home. You found it
dead on the verge of the lake road – tinier –
more fragile than you could have imagined – disguised
as fallen leaves in the wet grass – shabby
with soullessness – talons still gripping as though trying
to secure itself to a concept it couldn't
quite grasp. You returned by dark – gathered
its hollow-boned body in a plastic bag.

For so long you keep hope floating on a current
in the cooling air expecting to surprise
your infinite vision perched on a branch
by the light of an afternoon moon – alive
and seeking. Months go by without craft.
Your insight is sleeping a long winter sleep
in the frozen earth with the worms – unfeathering.
When it returns it will be something other –
imperishable – and beyond understanding.

At night I dream of the wings of my wisdom
spread out in my hands. I want it to fly at me
screeching – my wisdom – which is also my war.

Letter in October

'And I,
who only wished to keep looking out,
must now keep looking in.'
– *Ted Kooser*

When I was younger, I had an idea
of dystopia, a story begun with a story –
an elder telling tales at a fire, flames
dissecting her face into shadow and amber.
She would be the narrator. Young ones would sit
at her feet and listen. Her book would begin –
what I miss the most is the fruit, fresh fruit,
and coffee – I held this in my head, in my chest,
like something overheard, not dreamt.
Like all my fictions, I couldn't get past
the opening. Couldn't see where or how
to keep going. Never really tried. Now I sit
at my own quiet hearth, no young ones to preach to
of loss and excess, only us, and the world
isn't over, yet, though it feels like it's ending,
every day feels like something is ending.
We still have the coffee for now. We order
by post from an artisan roastery. It arrives
at our door like a promise of continuity.
Each morning we make a pot and drink it
slowly, savouring the flavours, the time,
this indulgence we offer ourselves.
But fruit is beyond me now. The factory
of my stomach shut down before the factory
of the earth. An irony I couldn't predict.
October, and each day the dark comes quicker,
more completely. In the imperfect mirror
of the living room window I catch myself –
the furred body blurring to twilight, turning
to return to the shivering woods – and the woman

inside the house bending over the fire,
face distorted as it flares, almost frightening,
downturned mouth moving, chewing the words –
what I miss the most is the fruit –

The tree in the wall dreams

of flight
of how sun moves around stone
of stripping themself down to their simplest arrangement

of conversation
of leaves so huge they blot out mountains
of bareness

of woods
of the pachydermal trunks of their elders
of being amongst others

of forest
something ancient their cells remember
and something future

the tangled burrowing dreams
of those who sleep in their roots and their skin
and channel thoughts through them

moonlight
raindrop
expansion
sap

of being one element of a body of many
of the dreams of the many they dream are dreaming
their dreams too

that leaves
instead of falling to earth
rise and turn to light

Moss Oak

'[I have been walking] in the dark woods … among my soft-sleeping brothers and sisters. Across the high moors among the sweet-scented ghosts of my brothers and sisters long dead. Under the grey sky through the dreams and murmurs of my brothers and sisters yet to come.'
– *Susanna Clarke*

That year I fell I love with a tree. How ridiculous
to not notice it before – the most lovely – the finest –
so solitary on its mossy island in the bog – yearning outward –
never reaching its neighbours – the upright families of beech and birch.

I watched it revolve – green sweeten to gold to brown – tumbling down
on itself – leaf-fall as mimic of deer-crunch – leaf confetti in a blaring sky.

I visited all through winter. Sometimes I stood and admired it at a distance.
Sometimes I picked my way through the mire – tussock to tussock
to whisper sweet nothings into its green furred trunk its branches
putting my hands on it – respectfully – kissing its roots.

I asked nothing of it but to allow me its presence.
Except its acceptance. Except its present.

I sat with it through bare times. Then summer pushed up
blockades of bracken – poured down rains
that sank the ways I knew to reach it.
I stood at a distance and sang to it – dear one –

wait for me through fraying autumn –

I'll come to you when the pathways are opened
by the falling off of the year –

and lie down in your soft green hold
like the deer do – under your wooden firmament –
sleeping giant in the miniature forest
of the moss – the sweet deep galaxies of moss

and if someone else walks back, what of it?
If they know the way – let them have it.

Considering A Haunting

All my life I've had it wrong.
I'm not saying this now because I watched
the small girl visited by her future self
in the moment of dying, an echo she read
as a haunting, a thing reaching forward from the past
and not a thing from beyond reaching back –
how you only know which way time is taking you
when you see yourself in the dress and grasp
you are your monster – a warning or just
a kind of randomised scrolling through moments
you catch on, on your way back down through your life
to the start – but sometimes you rewatch a memory
from the beginning of memory and it clicks, finally,
you reconsider a haunting with new
data and new data handling – like all
these years I've said grandmother could not parse
what species I was as I sat cross-legged
on the carpet at her feet – *little frog* – and she
declared to the assembled jury *what a nice*
little girl what a nice little boy what a nice
little cat dog all those years I thought
it meant she couldn't discern me as human
when just this hour I stepped into my ghost
and saw me in all my skins, beyond words –
(not) girl (not) boy (not) animal – neither –
every and none of the above.

The grey wagtail teaches

How to catch sun around your edges.
How to use it to flit up when everything pulls down.

Not to be afraid of cold water,
of the dark dome of winter.

That we are always carrying summer in our bellies
even when all we can see is the under
carriage of clouds with no visible seams.

That there is always joy, even if not
there when we go to call for it, even

if not in our bodies, when our bodies are tumbling
terrified through grey undifferentiated days,

that it has its own life outwith us. When we go
to air ourselves out, it will fly in bobbing.

How it nests in the simplest of movements, even
when we've given it up. How it spreads
by bending into its image.

Season 2

January

Velvet on antlers like moss on branches,
softening what is bare and cold.

In the season of antler growth the deer
are always eating.

No progress without rest
no growth without rest
no development without rest
no future without rest.

Make yourself a nest of the world,
scuff it up until it comforts you.

Lie down in the place you've made good for yourself.
Lie down in your good work and rest.

Inclement Weather for Immortal Hags

February comes in on a storm, wind
shaking the roof to its rotten core, slates
chattering. We are spare teeth compacted
in its jaw like enchanted sleepers. Trees
tapping at our panes with fingerbones loaned
from the dead, infecting our fractured dreams.
Everything screaming. All gale, no owl.
No one could rest through a night like this.
The day rises up like a flood, inevitable.
My ancestors shudder in my skin. We go out
not because the day is better,
but because the nights are worse. We go out
to move our blood. We meet three deer
on the common. We see a giant raven
carrying sticks in their beak. At the top
of our tiny world, a weak sun blinks
through cloud. The lightning rod of the white
birch I tied a red thread round
on this same day in an antique era
watching suspiciously with its many eyes.
The thread – a spell against loss, a plea
for mercy from the perilous realm – frays
into a sleety wind. Next year
it will vanish entirely. I won't notice for months.
It's not raining or snowing. It's not fine either.
The lake slate grey like a roof or wall
that would shut any mortal out.
Is it winter enough for an end to winter?
We declare inclement weather for immortal
hags. Aged as we have, a thousand
years in the turbulent dark, my crone
shadow on top of me now. We have
one foot in this place and one in another
and something is dragging at both of our hands.
I want to go home. I want to sleep through.
I want the cave and the torpor. I want
to take all these layers off and lie skin bared

to a parallel sky. Do immortal hags
feel their feelings? I'm feeling all mine.
We have left an offering of our sadness, our small
despairs poor fuel for her fire.

Prey Animals

Every afternoon I go to the woods
to be with the deer. The deer
are the only ones I care to be with.
I go quietly because they prefer me quiet.
I creep round the wall to the turf path in case
they are waiting for me. They dislike disturbance.
I walk towards the arras of trees
I know they are watching my progress from,
arms softly open to signal my good
intent. I have wanted to join them so long
but have known myself unworthy, clumsy
with hunger and all the wrong feelings for the dawn.
In the twenty-fifth month of the year of the plague,
the deer are my only hope of society.
I am getting better at being like them,
cautious and bold. I take a few steps
and stop, move my head back and forth
on my neck to be sure of the distance between us

– and I cannot distinguish if what I feel
in my ribs is the thud of red deer running
or the percussion of my quaking heart does it enter
through the feet or the throat what pulse is measured

you've struggled with this for years is the sigh
an owl perched high on the ridge or your laboured
breath a ghost of an owl in the chest
broken wings still beating for you –

The deer do not run from you now. They wait
for you to keep going. You nod and alter
your route. Is it because they smell
your gathering weakness or because they admit
your fellowship since you unveiled as prey –
as you always were – as you will always be?
Protected only until you trespass.
To be shielded, then to be culled.

Not Dying

Not dying is not the same as being
reborn. You may feel like it – shaking like a foal
after fever. Not dying might feel like life
but life is not not dying. It is merely
going on. There's no miracle in that. Coming to
and realising your heart is intact and not
gone off as you thought in the night – that your arm
has not exploded – your throat not closed –
that you passed through the pit of a hundred centuries
and rose up like the sun, a gold lion pawing
at your sickness, and yes, lying down is not dying
even when you would rather pull up the turf
to your chin like a blanket and sleep a long sleep
in the dark of the earth, starless, because
being upright is not not falling anymore
than falling is the same as failing, anymore
than the moon is sad because her mouth is open,
giving out what she has taken, as though not hoarding
what was never your own is generous. The moon
is no plagiarist. Only she can do what she does.
Nothing is made out of nothing.
We lie down, we get up. Something is lost
or gained. Or both. We are dying quicker
or slower than we think. This is my secret.
I keep passing myself from night to day
so a light is always shining.

The Private Life of the Poet

If I lie on the ground I think I think
they can't see me. I slump
flattening myself to the grass like the cat.
The bench beyond the veil of fence
faces me directly. If I crawl to the kitchen
maybe I avoid scrutiny. There is the horror
of being seen and the horror of being documented.
They hold their phones in their hands
as the tour begins.
                    Through the bars
you can see her. The bars are for her comfort.
She is not a danger. She will not bite.
But do not feed her. The bars give her the illusion
of a private life. But there is no privacy
in poetry, dripping from her forehead as she scribbles
in that notepad on her lap. See how she hunches
in focus. There is inspiration in progress!
At the Poetry Zoo: Home of Poetry
we guarantee inspiration. Please donate generously.
You will be supporting the upkeep of the Poet's Enclosure.
We like to keep things traditional for her:
peeling paint, leaky windows, broken
taps, holes in the roof through which rain
may enter, and swallows and the ghosts of dead poets
and poems swoop back and forth without ever
disturbing her work. Your donations support
the work of supporting the work. Yes
she's quite safe like that. Quite comfortable. No,
she doesn't even know we're here.

Frog Song

Today, I don't want to write about abandonment
or anger, about the limits of love,
or the invisible border where our worlds meet that dissolves
all mutual care – how to shed it, to go on
without it – is so much easier –

I want to write about a cool
scarf of water drawn over my body
I want to write the relief of sun
on my face, of feeling my whole self soften
under its touch, my cold hand trying
to catch it, to hold it, a golden ball
dropped into a well. If I capture it now
I will capture their hearts.
They will give me my selfdom.
They will welcome me into their gilded halls.

I want to bask in it, the bubble of light.
I want to grasp it between my palms
and crush it through my chest wall. I want it
burning its cleansing power at my core.
I want its truth throwing shade on everyone.

I want to believe in the undeniable
brilliance of frogs, in inalienable love.
Solidarity rising like mist from the water
lit from above. Weightless. Transcendent.
I want to believe in trust.

So Easily Offended

The problem with your generation
a man shouts at our intergenerational group
as we sit on the stony shore of the lake
the problem with your generation
whose conversation he has overheard
from the cover of the trees *the problem with your*
generation is you're so easily offended.
I had spoken aloud the fateful words
pretty offensive without thinking of the sensitive
ears of the other users of the shore.
The end of July. A cold snap after
a week of heat. We shivered celebrating
our time by the water. He had to speak out.
His peace was shattered by our taking offence.
We didn't shut up. We were laughing about it.

He was not wrong. I am easily offended.
I experience pain where others feel itching
or annoyance. In my floppy heart. In my bruising
flesh, my frangible bones. I was born
sensitive. I can pinpoint a dead thing rotting
in the undergrowth from metres away. My thin
skin is remade daily from my smallest
parts. It lets it all through. I was born
on a Wednesday. I was born to complaint. I was born
easily offended. I was born to say
that's not fair to a whole life giving
life isn't fair in reply. Life

isn't fair and I learnt not to cry because crying
is ugly. I drew my tears into my sensitive
body – a dark expanse in the gut –
spilling up, filling my sinuses with a pressure
undetectable on scans. It hurt but didn't
everything? I learnt to appease. I learnt
to laugh at softness. My own. Others'.
I learnt to destroy the things I love
because I couldn't destroy the things which offended.
I take things too seriously. I always have.

Days pass and I am taking the words
of the shouting man at the lake too seriously,
taking them too seriously as I stew in the bath,
as I gaze out the window at the August rain
as – from behind the safety screen
of my garden wall – I hear a child call
in the inflected wail of the easily offended
It's not funny. It's not funny. Don't laugh at my discomfort.
I hear you. I am over forty and still
a small child shouting through tears I cannot
stop – *don't laugh it's not funny don't laugh*
at my discomfort. It hurts.

Emergency Dream

There is a path where is it always autumn.

Step as soft as you can from the road
onto the track through the bracken, under

the moss branch into a different season

            you couldn't say when

even in this hottest summer in history –
the ponds dried up into crackle-glaze mud
and the ghostly trash of the age of industry
rising back up
            bog-bottles
                        bog-plates
            over it all a smell of burning –

the path of lichen and fox leaves is cool

and damp. Portal to the past. Dream
of forgiveness. Of rain and recovery. Dream

in which all of us get to thrive.

Silver Birch

On first glance, delicate.
Bone white so we glow
in the dark. Purple at our tips
in the naked season. Will root
in shallow ground, disturbed
earth. Make our own balance.

We turn glaciers to forest.
Hold the autumn
sun in our cores.
We are gold when we fall.

We shed our skin
like snakes. We scar
as we age.

Our sap is sweet
should you drink from us.

We are always watching
with our many eyes.

We see in all
directions.

Sessile Oak

a.k.a.
Not English.

Acorns like long-faced
ancestors in hand-knit
tams. I love
all the shapes of you.

A dream of a tree
sprouting from moss
and rock. The glowing
half-globe of you.

You have the look
of eternity. Look
of a passage. I love
to lean on you

and put my ear
to your fur and hear –
in the split leaflight –
beyond you.

The Owls Have Words

Each night this winter
owls circle
the house calling –
keewick – hoo hoo –
perch on the lintel,
on the chimney, talons
scratching the slates
over the rotten
roof timbers, line every
windowsill calling
            calling

for their lost one or
calling us out –

I don't know what
they are saying what
they want from us
            or her –
all night calling
so close I think
they are in the room with us
looking down
from the shadows of the wardrobe –

in the thick half light
of day I study
the glass for the print
of their beaks pressing in –

I buried her voice.
Can she no longer call to them?

I dug up her skull
a little too late
ill-practised at exhumation – small
bones softening and splitting, beak
cracked at the base,
jaw dislocating.

I mistook her jawbone
for a wishbone as though
she could snap some thought
into being by speaking.

Each night, all night
they surround us, calling.

I want to explain
I loved her too.
I carried her home
to keep her near.
I wanted to save
something of her. Sad
and angry, and afraid
to lose her, to lose
what she meant, afraid
for myself, selfish
in the ways of my kind.

What do I know
of the wisdom of owls?

Maybe I took her death
from them.

Maybe they searched
for months for a sign
to explain her loss.
Maybe they need her
to let them move on.
Maybe this vigil
is grief. Maybe
acceptance. Maybe
hunger. Now

the owls sound sad –
sad more than angry –
though I don't know the words
they are using as they claw
round the house each night
all night, calling
                    calling

            lost one
            you have lain
            too long
            in the earth

            in the sodden earth
            unflighting. We are here
            to remind you
            of a different
            quality of dark

Season 3

Resolving

To turn my face to the sun at every opportunity.
To wash in its gold like the cat does. To choose
light over productivity. Comfort
over productivity. To be kindly with myself.
To break into simpler parts. To loosen.
The moth-holed clouds of the old year blown open
to let the moon shine through. To vanquish
abstemiousness. Against deprivation.

I will weather these months as the deer do, eating
and resting when I will. Putting all of my store
into personal growth, turning the winter
into velvet and bone, and my own survival.

I will practise my big antler energy. Towards
resting red deer face, the furrow in my brow
less of a comment than a natural phenomenon
and when I am threatened I will leap free and vanish
and when I am threatened I will leap free and vanish
and the space I abandon will be less-than without me.

I am filling my pockets with all the sun I can carry
and turning them out in the burrow of the house
at twilight. I am being lavish with my logs
even before dark, if the day is too dark,
though there's so much winter to burn through.

I am taking it one fire at a time
against the daily emergency of this endless
heedless season of gloom. I am cleaning
my bones. I am lighting all my candles.
I have given up giving up.

Cat in February

I wanted my face in the sun –
catself – triumphant and uncorruptible
in my half sleep – eyes
half open – body
entirely surrendered to the earth entirely
ready to run –

but crawled into slow worm
curled into the hollow interstices of the wall –
a curved branch
turning myself to stone and lichen –
tessellating skin
caramelising in unexpected warmth –

the sun like a chink in the wall of winter
blue sky like a chink in the wall of winter

got sundrunk – forgot myself –
tangled in silvers –
misled by my own shadow
ahead of me on the wall – fell into
purring slumber –
lost all pounce

sun like a chink in the wall of winter
blue sky like a chink in the wall of winter

Optometrist/Plague Year Season 3

The closest I've been to a stranger in months –
the year-long months of plague time – the optometrist
shows me maps in the backs of my eyes. We are flying low
over river systems in an orange earth, through deciduous
woods in winter, parallel to the ground, thin dark
branches static in frozen air, amber
sun dropping down to relieve them. We stepped

over the threshold of the mirror world
and it unfolded its geometries before us, travelers
in a stranger dimension. I don't remember
having been here before, but it's been so long
since anyone looked deep into my eyes, longer
since anyone cast my own secrets back to me.

The optometrist says it's a treat to visit –
she rarely sees humour so youthful, so bold –
it softens over years, she explains, whilst I'm thinking
of myself as antique as the fantasy geologies
my blood has carved out through the canyons of jelly,
the folly of it, the colossal wreck of it all.

When I leave my eyes are as big as planets
and the light is too much to take in.

The Limits of Music as Time Travel

Increasingly I find time is folding in on itself –
a strain in a minor key with a modal shift and I'm
looking forward again, from a different century
pinned to the floor by the weight of history
which belongs to me only in the sense that all
history does – a train on a dress
I've been told to put on – catching on everything –
but able to imagine a future in which
I could dance a bit lighter, wearing myself
like an airy cloud. Is this how it is
midway, to be stuck in the mud of the present,
unable to see further than the first of the bends
in the road, so dreaming backward, trying
to recapture that feeling of carrying the sadness
in one hand, the hope in the other? So often
it is music that does it. How you'd lie on the carpet
and weep or walk in circles round the room
with the lights out transported by your Walkman
whilst everyone else was out or asleep,
Relieving you of your floundering self. Now
when you listen it is her you hear, brimming
with misery and wonder and fury. Is this
as far as the tape can loop? I am spooling
out of time, an ancient technology.
My obsolescence sings in the wind.
I am older today than the first of the flutes
some ancestor whittled from the bone of a kill.

Pain Metaphors

Back to school again with the plaster off
I tripped and fell in the classroom. I was tripped
in the classroom, and fell. In so much pain.
Those days I told mum it felt like just crossing
the classroom was walking through treacle.
Like trying to run in a dream when your body
won't let you won't move but it wasn't a dream
my body wouldn't let me. My body was trapped
moving through the treacle of the day. The day
moving through the field of my body turned all
the ordinary world to treacle. My foot
stuck in the treacle of the classroom carpet
and I fell. And because I hurt, I hurt.
And because they laughed, my friends, at the way
I cried, I knew it wasn't their lives.
I was in a different story. A world
of treacle, like the game that L and I played
where the carpets were made of lava. They thought
I was being a baby. They thought I was crying
over nothing. And all I felt was pain,
so much pain of everything, of the unhealed
tissue of my broken ligaments jarring
as I fell, of the shame of my weakness, of the way
the girls I thought were my friends kept laughing,
laughing and laughing as I cried.

Petroglyph Way

2010

For Ulrike and Frank

When I landed they said the smoke from the fires
was making the sky heavy. Forested
mountains screened by white. Tonight
it oozed a magnificent lilac, the giant
sunflowers inching away with the light.
My feet are filthy and have been for days.
Buddy is barking on the side-deck and the moon
is a single headlamp flickering between trees
behind the house – the old kind – yellow
and blurry. Down Darby the cows are bellowing
back at the first star's thin high murmur
calling more stars forward like the small
deer stepping out of the woods.
That liminal place the road is,
concrete at the edge of vision.
Stars. Deer. Contentment. Catastrophe
distant and looming as the moon.
At home, it is already tomorrow.
Tomorrow, I start to go home
where the fire sleeps
like a prophet under peat
dreaming the blaze to come.

Thirty

That summer I was living at home, where home
means a place you thought you'd moved away from.
I was falling down in the street, I was shaking,
I was sick. I was broke. I was turning thirty.
I was shrinking the landscapes of my childhood, I was treading
in my own worn footprints, laying myself down
in a shape my body once wore on a lawn.
I was acting up. I was dressing up
as an adult – as myself at fifteen – as Byron –
a bride in a veiled pillbox hat – a magician.
I was matching my colours like a spell.
I was photographing mould like a project for school.
I was learning the names of parking attendants.
I started to believe my beloved was a cat.
I started to believe the cat was a fiction.
I was swimming my thoughts away like I used to
stroke by deliberated stroke.
I was dreaming of growing up, where up
is a job and a place you have chosen, a life,
the means to make growth happen. I was moving
papers and books from room to room –
an elaborate shuffle – I was cutting the deck
as though this would cause revolution. I was held
on pause, worn and crackling. I was singing
but no one would listen. I was summer. I was living
but barely. My world in boxes shoved under
a bed I could not call mine. I was thinking
this is just the caesura   waiting
for a form to pour into, waiting for a volta
to turn it to something that mattered.

All My Litter

A rocky cove on an island far from home.
White pebbles, sun-bleached driftwood.
Shattered pines like signs for something.

I watch purple starfish move in clear water.
Everything is moving, if you look carefully enough,
for long enough. Nothing is still.

Not me, for sure, though I seem to sit paused
at rest. Not the waves at my toes, not the stone.
It's a matter of scale, of thinking outwith

this body, this life. Water rolling
rock to sand saying *shhhhh shhhhhhhh*
and gulls exciting. Across the bay

a ferry honking, enormous goose.
Salt and iron on my tongue. Ash
and smoke of distant forests burning

and factory belch on the next island over,
and something dead, much closer. Seaweed
and sea-glass and fag-ends and feathers. Light

enters my body through each open pore
and so do the fumes. This is not my air.
I am passing through, between engagements.

This beach, I mean, but also this timeline.
I am jetsam tangled in the wrack. I am vast
and slow as the rock of the shield beneath me.

I don't know why I have brought myself here
if not to dwell on that sameness and difference.
The hand-painted sign, its ripening brambles –

All my litter I will take thee home

Lack of Light in August

This is August the conjurer – summer
vanishes into tanks of rain – I read
we know things truly only as they're leaving –

incessant rain insisting rain
owls all night and toads in the walls
and suffering from lack of light in August –

a bad forecast for the coming months. In this house
the sun is a passage visitor. It does not
settle. The panic I feel at each clouded

day is directly proportional to the advance
of shadow across this North-facing patch
we rent from the woods. In this time of plague

the garden is my planet. We wake to gold
curtains on the cusp of Virgo season
and the shade of the house meets the wall at the limit

of my map. By noon there's illumination
deep enough to bathe in. It loiters
till four when it slinks through the door of the yew.

Light is leaving me. This is no metaphor.
At a rate I will never get used to. Each year
it is crueller, watching it go from me, knowing

we will live so comfortless all through the hardest
season – chasing the tiniest gleam
of mercy from room to room.

Cat in September

Blue sky breathing, the cat
pinning me to the bed till the sun clawed over

the ridge of the roof, so when I rose
the wall of the garden was dappled leaflight,

the little apple tree arched with the weight
of glowing green apples. Two hours to ease

into the day before anyone expected me,
melting the block of my muscle and bone

the yellow butter of my body softening
into the yellow butter of the sun.

Fox/Plague Year Season 3

First fox in years. Four in the morning,
crossing the lake road, carefully glancing
in both directions before she stepped out,
confident in the winter night, ours
the only car on the road and plenty
of time to pass before we reached her.
Road-safe Fox. Warning Fox.
Fox in command of personal responsibility.
We were on the way to the airport – my beloved
driving – me the one flying, crossing
the world on a wind of sickness. Ever
had your beloved drive you to the airport
for the season finale of a plague show when most
of the cast have forgotten the plot? I was shaking
like a rabbit in the careless beam of their glaring
denial. And when I most needed her, Fox
saying *courage! keep fleet, keep your own bristling council,*
keep your eyes sharp, your head down, keep wearing your mask
and you'll make it back. In the desert I meet
the skull of her cousin – white flag in the sand –
a message about distress and endurance. All through
the lonely journey I keep Fox in mind.
Her confidence in her prudent position. Her refusal
of shame. I wear it as though my future
relied on it. Without guilt. I make it back safe.

Season 4

Antler Revolution

I find you in leafmould and woodsmoke, your scent
of the long night, scent of survival, pelt

like the lining of a cobnut, protecting a universe.
You have dug a bed in the bracken as a moss

manifesto, a cushion I would rest on. You wait
like something important to be said. I would

go with you into the wood, believe
we could make something there. An antler revolution

determined by loss and revival, dispersal
of our bodies into hostile space, receptors

built of blood and energy. I am ready
for the shedding of the old. I think of it often.

Of growing a new more sensitive world
in place of last year's tatters. I am sprouting

into pedicle. Antenna. Rebellion. The expanded
self that could rise from my own tired skull

year after year after year.

Affirmation

I believe things are growing
even when we cannot see them.
Bulbs in the earth. Antlers in the wood.
I believe in information beyond our processing.
Networks fizzing through the dirt. That stone
is breathing, that air is heavy. I believe
in the agency of water. I believe in persistence
of life in the icebound stream. I believe
in the cells of bare trees sweetening. I believe
in dormancy. I believe it is good to lie down
and good to rise up, stretching. I believe
in slowness. I believe in the whole of the moon.
In the limits of the planet. I believe in the light
of all the suns burning in the vastness of space.

February. Month of mud. Our sun
removed for ritual cleansing. So far
from warmth in either direction it is hard
to imagine its touch on my skin. I try
to believe one day I will open my door to it.

For now, I believe in snowdrops. I believe
in their small white tablets splitting to stars
of green. Flaring constellations in the dark
firmament of lonely graveyards. I believe
in renewal. Snowdrops as the bones of the dead.
Snowdrops as wisdom teeth chewing the cud
of winter. I believe they will gnaw a hole in it,
enough for spring to creep through.

Pain Parade

Sometimes pain comes in in a parade, waving banners,
a hand held out before it as if to halt all traffic, as if
to say STOP little pigeon, I will take it from here, I am pain!

Pain wears a head like a moth and the body of an owl.
Pain's feet bend the wrong way. Pain
appears to be looking ahead but that's gaze
misdirection, to confuse pain's predators. Pain
has a mouth like a star, a head split in two.
Is purple and green like a bruise. Pain
carries a pennant as if expecting a tournament.

The flag, of course, is red, like the sky
is red, a throbbing red, as if
one of its many faces bled out.

Sometimes pain is a bright green dragon
on a ghostly diadem, floating out of itself,
a huge egg concealed in the crawl space which may
or may not belong to the pain. Pain
is a unicorn, or a white charger, head
hidden in a canopy of spiralling portals.
Pain wears a pink ribbon round its moonlight neck

so you don't get lost when it carries you away,
though there is nothing solid to tie it to. In the distance,
trees, and the hint of a forest beyond –

and sometimes pain is a spectral labyrinth,
haunting all hours, walls like spokes
of a wheel, separating the woman, the child,
the horse, the bull, the pageant.

Declaration/Plague Year Season 4

I am here to declare my own preciousness. My life
is precious, my existence is precious. My skin
and the organs it holds in are precious. My blood
is precious as water is precious. My skull
is precious as an unmined seam of gold
and the lake above it, and the creatures within it,
thriving in their lack of industry, wild
with belief in their own high value. And my brain
is precious, wild and precious, its synapses,
all of its chemical life, its costly
cells, teeming with preciousness. I am
as important as the most important of people
you think of as precious to you are. Precious
as the rarest of orchids. As the most charismatic
of megafauna, extinct or at risk,
the ones you would save, the ones you would clone.
Their lives, too, precious. As precious as the rocks
of my eyes, huge with pleading. As the last
of my kind. As any one life. I am here
to tell you. I value myself. Value
this too. I have no intention of surrendering
the bramble of my precious life, its fruit
and its spines, irrepressible juice, the fox
and cubs of my precious life, bright
and uninvited, the tiny proliferating
alpine strawberry of my continued existence.
Its sweetness. The biting horsefly of my heart.
The dandelion clock of my heart. Dispersed
on your breath. A careless wish. The sole
precious white foxglove of my heart.

Treelight

what I would give to bottle the light
on a June evening   an evening in early
June   the sun a late arrival
splitting through trees still spangled from weeks
of rain   and the world   the world incandescent
green   greenish   treelight and honey

what would I give?
                    the heart in winter?
the rain in August?
                                        a bearable future?

I'll not make a trade that will bud to a curse

just give me more June   more elderflower evenings
give me treelight   give me green   give me warmth on my skin
give me swallows on the line   when you'd lost all hope for them
let me keep it   through the dark   to come

Notebooks

My old notebooks are full of unfinished   I keep
a lot of notebooks a lot of unfinished

the notebooks swim around the house
on invisible currents   hidden in them

they cannot all be present at once

novels and nicknacks tumble from the shelves
bruise my cheekbone   I know the weight

of the right one in my grip   the colour of ink
the fragment is written in (turquoise)   the room

where I wrote it (before
the class settled). It was autumn
or spring. The room

white and too long.
The sound was not working.
The word I snagged on
was 'faltering'. The chill

of the rhythm shift.
A fox on a lawn
with two cats watching
from the window. The pages

plain, not lined.
I prefer that. Smaller
than average. I can see it
myself   materialising
stalled

If a poem were a time machine
as I said in that room as I wrote on the whiteboard

I could push my arm through the fringe of the scene
and pull the book through. Maybe I have.

If this sounds like an anxiety dream you haven't
seen how disordered my rooms are   how each

word dissolves in unrepresentative
language like the one I spoke

until they replaced it.

The Long Journey Out of the Self

After Theodore Roethke

On the long journey out I am wary of detours,
always fearful to find myself stranded
far from the place I intended. Nothing
to work with. Puttered and stalled. Still grey
from a long wet winter in this season I insist
on calling late summer. I almost have it,
the summit. I can almost see over the ridge.
My ankle turns. Shale slips under
my feet. Knee twists. You can't get out
however you scramble. The narrow path
vanishes into the rockface, replaced
by a rowan heavy with orange berries.
A single buzzard circles overhead,
keening. You are not chosen. The mountain
will not open. You must dwell in the fine
valley you have made your home.

Critics

Suddenly I think of the Dublin boy
who told me I wasn't a poet because
when I spoke my poems my poems didn't
rhyme or climb to some invisible measure
he held in mind as Poetry. In a bar
in Dublin he made me recite my poems,
told me I wasn't a poet and kissed me.
It is easy enough to forget that injury
twenty years on. A petty thing.
Later that night he offered to rape me
asked would I notice if he just slipped it in
and I spent the small hours awake in the kitchen
alone, till his sister woke up for work
and found me sitting there, shivering, alert.
Then we all climbed into his housemate's car,
me, my friend and the boy she followed
back to their house, and the critic, and the friend
with the car who drove us all to our hostel
to fetch our bags and on to the airport
singing U2 at the top of our voices
in a way that felt joyful and real. I wonder
if he's thought of it since as I have. The critic.
The way I deflected my anger – once
we were home and safe – at my friend because
I couldn't deliver it to his door.

Night Owl Version

In this version, the night and I are in cahoots. The moon
gives me permission to do what I need to.
She offers me her light, as it has been offered to her,
to use as I will. We are floodlight and mirror.

Out of our generous gaze spill bats and badgers, owls, foxes, all
the wild night things of the wood and field
and at last – ah yes, there he is after all –
the great stag, the most of it, antlers gleaming
with kinship in our full-beam attention.

A Message

A child was born – who meant hope –
meant something about grace and truth –
and a leader so eager to snuff out that message
set out to kill every single child born
in that land at that time, each child that could be
the child he believed posed a threat just by being –
some words, some flesh, some inherited meaning –
a child but also a metaphor – as all
children became through proximity – by being
born, displaced. By being born stateless.
Does this sound familiar? Do bells ring out?
They say there are no new stories, only
new ways of telling the oldest. Tonight,
the sky cleared briefly in a pause of the storm
that has shaken our home for days and one
bright star glared down for one cold moment
before clouds hid it again. Do you see
what I see? Listen. A child was born
in Bethlehem, in Palestine –
though they used a different name then, different
tyrants set the taxes – we're still
recycling the same old verses – and more
abided through these two thousand years
of wrong than repeating song – life's crushing
load, the nations still at war,
the weary world in error pining –
and sometimes a storm cloud parting at just
the second your hope is burning lowest
to reveal the same light falling, still,
silent, into the dreamless dark.
Don't tell me hope is a ghost. Any star
we can see is far from dying. So much
we take as gospel is apocryphal. A message
travels the little town of our galaxy
and 10,000 years of fear go by

before its patient splendour meets
our wondering eyes. Do you feel the worth
of the soul? Whose soul? All of the souls
on earth? O fall to your knees. O hear
the strife. O hush. O cease.

Season 5

A Flame in Winter

You need a flame in winter. Today
brings an ochre sun oozing low in the sky,
and a wind that howls through the valleys, through
the gullies of your ears. One hurt you feel,
the other you sense as pattern, copper
leaves and all your thoughts spiraling.

You take them to a pause between crags – a moss
swathed tree and a slab of sunwarm stone
where the wind is forbidden. Take off your hat.
You can listen now. Slip your arms from your coat.
Turn your face to the sun. There is love in it yet.
Little heart. Little pilot light in the short
hours when hope may be lit from it. Just
sit. Just sit. Just sit with it.

Larch

This seed
I can't name.
Dried husk
of a finished spring.
Snapped twig
of potential. Branch-line
of fate, cut off, dead end. I know
its sort, in general.

Grows on trees
like so many destinies.

I want to say *incomer.*
I want to say *plantation.*

I see it pink
and glowing, backlit
by low spring sun
flaring.

I call it *possibility.* I call it
Not Over. Yet. But

I won't plant it. It doesn't
belong to me. I balance
the broken stem
between my left
index finger and right. No
lightning bolt of creation. I guess
its history. Leave it unspoken.

Pain Logics

if you breathe through the pain they assume that the pain
is minimal

if you breathe through the pain, don't kick them away, they
assume that the pain is minimal

if you breathe through the pain, don't kick them away,
don't faint they assume that the pain is minimal

if you breathe through the pain, don't kick them, don't faint, don't
scream, they assume that the pain is minimal

they never consider the painstaking practice
it takes to become a pain professional

your original contribution to knowledge, champion
of distraction, oracle of embodied and dis

embodied cognition, enchanter shifting
planets and theorems as you lay on your back

on the torn paper sheet
on the table

Garden Version

In this version every owl has their own garden.
The billionaires have boarded up their windows against
a wilder generation, relinquished their claims
on their feral fiefdoms. Nothing belonged to them
anyway. There is a profusion of owls
in the absence of visiting billionaires. A profusion
of voles. A surplus of under-used gardens.
Every garden has an owl of its own. Every owl
a garden – although they don't call them that –
gardens – in this version – home.

Cold Long Day

There is the lightening half
and the darkening half.

This is how it is then.
Nothing to do but keep going through it.

Cold long day.
Light short night.
Little difference between them.

The further stars are coming toward you.
Owls call but you cannot see them.

Here on the road it is deepening to blue
but on the horizon the cloud is glowing
like the smooth opal back of a shell.

Turn your cold face to the rising moon.
Tomorrow it will be full.

As I lay down on the grass, I observed

After Sylvia Plath, after Edna St. Vincent Millay, after Annette von Droste-Hülshoff, After Dorothy Wordsworth, After Anon

All year I have been longing to lay myself down
in long grass, long grass in the sun casting

its green shadows over my toasting skin
so bee-flies and butterflies doze on my sticky
limbs and dragonflies skim my eyelashes

and I am a plant amongst plants. The grass
is long and full of life. The grass
is long and full of death. Ticks.

Weeds. Human Suffering. The mower
trapped in the shed by the scaffolding. All the dazed

year I have failed, reelingly vertical,
frenzied with the whirl of the world, groggy
with transience translated in my blood into woozy

longing for the rapture you wrote of. The daring
halt. Euphoric/fevered. I want

spine to ground, each cell down-reaching,
my bones dissolving into moss and dandelions,
self-heal and celandines, between the tall
drystone wall and the little apple tree
hidden from human uprightness, the greatest

surface of our body touching the body
of the earth touching the voice of the air /
the voice of the water in the air / the voice
of the trees in the earth /the voice of the grass /
the voice of the grass / the voice of the first

yellow leaves falling oh friends birds
so near unseen all the dead in my chest

all the dead let me I beg be bold
enough to keep my heart wakeful

I will not close my eyes for peace
I will not close my eyes for peace

there are other ways to be useful

and yet I fain would lie in this grass
sweet grass sweet dizzy sweet care sweet kiss
of hot dry dust I would roll in it follow
the beam of its light

            I am tired, so tired

it is hard, after all, to talk of rest
from travel, weary, and not mean end,
of lying down and not mean finally
of *green green grass* without *growing over me*
of turf without grave of dig without buried
of trench without corpse of dirt without death

sweet growth sweet growing
sweet deep deep flood
sweet tired, swimming head

I will lay you down
and open you up to the sky you love
and when we have talked it all through with the stars
radiance of migrating space-rubble marking
a different path
I will raise you back up
and float you onward
float on into splendour

that shimmering line
half-glimpsed through the woods
is not the border between this and the next
but the lake, deep enough to hold all
our tears and not spill over, clear
and steady enough to show you yourself
above and beneath the mirror, a rock
amongst rocks a tree amongst trees. Yes

lie down. You prefer it that way. More natural.
Lie down, and then swim on.

High Dam, Mid-September

We go up through the shadow forest of late afternoon,
passing the day's heat as it walks back down

re-meet the sun at the top, split
into filaments of alternate timelines by the dense

prism of the trees. The tarn is lit
on this side only, the sun a ball

balanced on the terminal buds of the pines
on the opposite shore. We don't have long.

I strip. Climb in. Part the cusp
of the season with my palms. All the colours

I cling to wrinkle and marble – blue
and gold green gold red gold clear amber,

a backlit honey I would store in jars
against winter – and fold into black.

Bright warm surface. Deep cold under.
All still water is a scrying mirror.

I shiver as I travel. My love I told you
up here was something like Canada. I swim

across oceans. I swim in Ontario alongside
J and the snapping turtles, through myself

up here one burning summer, A's face
and mine as water lilies, glowing

and waxy. This evening the sun is scattering
into infinite potential as it exits. I float

in the last of it, blazing, watching the dark
advancing over the glass of the water.

There is such a cold dark coming. There is grief
deeper than the deep cold centre. I can see

my breath in it now as I swim back toward you,
you and the shore in twilight already.

Above, the sky, still blue and gold
with the fullest of harvest moons rising.

Cat in October

Should you return as a cat at my window
in an autumn storm I would let you in

I would let you in when you knock on the glass
with your claws I would let you

into my life. Reshape it around
the length of you

your plaintive requests
for companionship

your demand for absolute
comfort. I would learn

to be more like you.
Hesitant to trust.

Giving my trust
completely. Always

knowing the best
place to sleep.

Autumn Song

Days like today, I learn love for autumn,
all our fur warm in the sun and the leaves
stained glass windows to a brighter dimension.
More like this and I could accept
the way they shorten quicker than my blood
can grasp, the furthering dark, the mist
in the hollows erasing roads I cannot
follow. I could lie fallow in sun
like this, think gentle thoughts about time
and seasons and *couldn't we all love this earth*
and each other? On days like this I believe
it could happen how could you not when the world
is so golden so good so radiant with hope
for regrowth even as it loosens its hold
on what it no longer needs and frees it.
So basic to look at these reeling leaves
and see death instead of survival. Forgive me.
All those decades I held you accountable
for my limited scope of perception. So much
mourning in place of celebration. Autumn,
will you let me lie down in your burnishing arms?
Will you tell me how spring is within?

Burying The Cat

Blood at her mouth like she'd taken someone with her

twenty-four mild December hours
since they handed me her body, swaddled in a soft
synthetic blanket, sealed with masking tape

blood at her mouth like a kill and a chain
of ice at her neck, a ceremonial collar
to mark her status
                    though she hated the cold.

She never liked to be covered over.

I thought of this as I packed down the damp
earth above her.
                    She got lonely in the dark

but the earth is no quilt and the dark of it different
to the dark of a lonesome nighthouse to the live
and anxiously mortal.
                          I was the animal
who needed to hold her body to believe
she was gone.
                  The night before, digging the grave
in the dark and rain like a scene from a thriller
in which I was digging my own, the pain
felt like meditation.

I laid some part of myself in there with her
and covered us over all the same, the fierce
and unrelenting part of me, something
that would not bend to anyone's will

that knew myself sovereign of all I encountered
that would hold on for the kill.
                                          That would sleep
all day paws over my eyes. That would come home
singing. That resisted all assistance.

I laid it with her, to rest in communion
with the bones of her venerable adversaries, honour
in death.
            What was left of us – softer, less certain.
Concerned with comfort. With solace, with keeping
all our best loved ones in sight.

Self Portrait as Didi

After Megan Fletcher

In this version I am a deer. I have grown
stubby two-pronged antlers on my roebuck
head through a winter I will not talk of.
One of my eyes is a round dark mirror.
One of my eyes is a binary star.
I walk on two legs, stand upright, like
a human with the head of a deer, hands
like a human, feet like a human, torso
in slices like vertebrae, gaps where the spinal
column and organs should be. You can see
right through me, if you get the right angle. Or
the absence that allows me to function. I am
built from scraps and the colour of lichen
on bark, of the depths of the lake. I wear
a shift like a veil strung with charms. One truth:
what moves me is out of my body. I am stuck
on repeat, overlapping myself. I am tumbling
through my own image and centuries. Sinking
to rock. At rest in the bed of the wood.
Isn't this what I wanted? To embody
wild-deerness. Iconic. Time told in antler.
I am loosely strung. I fall as being.
The two star system of my right eye forming
its own gravitational field. Half
my face is night sky and asterism. I am
accelerating out through the page.

Season 6

Glow Up

I met a fox at the edge of a bluebell
wood who walked me down into winter

through sunlight and moonlight into the dark
underearth of the woods lit

by stars that were not stars but hearts
blazing in a spreading galaxy. Fox

laid their red muzzle on my shoulder. We rested
until our breath became tiny lamps floating

in and out of our bodies and knew
we'd developed beyond incandescence. Later

when we stand on the familiar path through the wood
and I can't see the ground at my feet it's ourselves

we pull glowing from our pockets.
Ourselves that light the way on.

Sing The Things You See

I.M. Jamie Normington

How unlike you to be dead.
Didn't you have a pile of books
to be read you'd not got through yet? Weren't you
on your way to a book launch, on your way to a wood,
on your way to introduce a friend
to a tree? To give a stranger a gift
to ease their journey? To make a stranger
a friend? A friend an ally? To build
a home for birds? To teach us all
gently about wildness and memory, a lesson
about action and restoration? Aren't you
about to arrive any moment, laughing
with a tale of where you've been?

The last time I saw you the sun was shining
for the first time this spring it seemed. Perhaps
I'm remembering wrong. I was driving. You were walking
out of a different part of the hospital
I had just left. You were swinging a white
plastic bag in your hand. I shouted
your name to the car in surprise. I waved
from the wheel but you didn't see me. I almost
reversed round the one-way system thinking
I'd draw up beside you. In the rear-view mirror
you looked contained, your focus turned inward
as though singing a song to yourself of things
I could not see, carrying you forward
through clear spring light, as though you had
somewhere important you meant to get to
and I didn't want to interrupt you.

Year of Dragons

Never before a May so bright so dry –
never a year of so many dragons –
dragons of air and light –

skimming the surface of the lake – bellies
ignited by evening sun – sun
on the year's young leaves the colour of dragons –
the low evening sun on the fresh green leaves
of the trees reflecting in the flickering surface
of the lake the colour of dragons – lamé
fuselage seen from the cool inner workings
of the lake – say by a swimmer – only
a head in the water like an untethered buoy –
blue-green engines of future so brilliant
I forget they are predators – hawk and hawker –
iridescent warriors –
drone and dive –

how they halt
mid-flight – reverse
to lock their target
in their sight –

dragons circling my head – swans
circling the lake – the lake all diving
mergansers and wagtails flitting and damselflies
blue as the sky and dragons patrolling –

dragons of air and light and hunger

so still in their motion to my motion – something
I've forgotten about fulcrums – dragons retaining
all the light of new growth in their radiant
armour – the brightest May I remember –

my body so glad of the clarity – the pause
in the scrutiny of heat – I am generating summer
in my flight muscles – turning the sun to a promise
or threat – this month of dragons orbiting
my head as I swim every evening – reporting
their news of short lives, precarity, violence –
my head all dust motes and fragments – they weigh
a soul against the unstable season –
they know what is true, what is lies.

Dreaming the Owls

I went to look for you where my dream located you,
that old favourite spot where the rock makes a gully
in the wood. In my sleep it spread, a forested
chasm of hidden growth concealed
by our home which you entered by turning your trust
it was there in the lock of a trunk. Place
unfolded by conscious presence. There
perched between moss and slate, owlets.
Ghostly and actual. I am here. I am waiting.
I am ready when you are ready to branch
into material space, be known
as real in the wealth of your realness. I am
adjusting my vision. I am standing where the bracken
grows over my head for you. The blackbird alarm
louder and louder. I am wide awake
with faith, fronds tickling my chin. I am scouring
the trees for you in the last of the light.
Night will arrive soon enough.

True Poetry

After Auden, After Cooper, After Jamieson, After Joudah, After Anon

'Unlike politics, true poetry is not broad brush. It is probing, open-minded, delicate and full of surprise'.
– *Anon*

'I woke up, and it was political'.
– *Jamieson*

True Poetry would like a word with you but
it's too busy being indelicately political
political in its marrow / punctuation / its line
breaks a statement that cannot be
denied its capitals or lack of capitals
too – full of surprise. It mines / under
mines. It goes beneath surfaces, unseen,
burrowing beneath the opened skin
of the language. Silly, like us, with meaning.
It keeps on happening. Mouthing mouthing.
It keeps on waking. It keeps on walking
its disconsolate political lines, as though
to speak is a means of surviving. It keeps on
believing it means. Translating its trueness.
When it sleeps, we all dream its dreams.

Pain Metaphors

Dad asks why I was trying last night
to get into his grandmother's garden, patrolling
the hedge, which was growing and growing as I searched
for a gap in the tangle to push through, chickens
eight decades dead pecking my feet
and chasing me off. I began at my usual
size, he said, but by the time
he lifted me out of the brambles, I was
small and cold so cold he was scared
I would never get warm. In the house the bath
is already run, just the right measure
to bring me back. He doesn't say
I thought you were dead. Instead, *I thought*
you would never get warm. We know what that means.
As for the rest, the chickens, the hedge?
His dream translates my pain / our pain.
He is living a slow recovery, a bad thing
pulled from his leg in the Spring. I tell him
he saved me. He says *you were just so cold*
so cold and you almost weighed nothing. I thought
you would never get warm. I don't say outside
the dream you cannot carry me. I don't say
what was I doing at your grandmother's house?
A fox in the garden, shrinking out
of my life. I don't say wasn't it lucky
the house or somebody in it was ready
before us, knew what we'd need when at last
we arrive. One of us lighter than ever.
One of us bearing the weight.

Ottering

There are otters in the lake.
I haven't seen them.

I haven't seen them
but I know they're there.

When I'm swimming I'm sharing
the water with otters

even though I don't see them.
I haven't seen them.

I know they're there.
Do I need to see them?

I know they're there, being their otter
selves, doing the things of otters.

I trust the reports of otters. I trust
others who have seen the otters are neither

lying nor mistaken when they say they've seen otters
in the lake, in the river, swimming right past

the school when the school is closed, scrambling
up the drystone bank of the beck

by the pub, leaping from a jetty, playing
in empty boats where the river enters

the mere, rolling in the reeds, rolling
and diving in the water where I roll and dive

like an otter, in the water where I turn onto
my back and float with my paws up drifting

in a pose I have learnt to call *ottering*. Sun
behind clouds. Moon in the day. Otters

in the lake. It doesn't need faith. It doesn't
need proof. I know they're there. No words

I can utter will make them show themselves.
No words I delete can make them vanish.

Although the rate of otter fraud
is less than 0.0%

and fewer than 0.4%
of otters are wrongly accounted

some people will not believe in an otter
they have not seen for themselves in the water.

You can monitor a lake for decades, study
its history, closely observe its movements,

swim in it week after week through every
season, through ice and rain and drought

miss its otters. I live this truth
in my body, as I float on my back in the centre,

paws on my chest, ottering, in
the presence of unseen others.

Green Abundance

It is June. The woods are getting maximalist
and why shouldn't we? Let our words grow over
the trodden paths of winter, let our leaves
eat the light. Be dapple be chatter be tendrils
be branches reclaiming their space, be spiraling
foxglove, be bee, be blossom, be bilberry
purple with midlife extravagance. Let us
bend to the earth with the weight of our fruitfulness.
Let us swallow all travelers on our ground in our green.

It's impossible to have enough of it, the light
of midsummer. This brief luxuriance, just
as the year begins to comprehend
itself in all its variousness. Be
everything with me. Be extra. Be excess.
Be flower. Be flourish. Be much. Be more.
Be bursting to bloom on bloom on bloom.
There is nothing surplus to this green abundance.
How else are we ever meant to live with the fall?

Yew

Each day I watch
the clock of your shadow

turn the world
toward night

I have thought of you
as an agent of sorrow

I have thought of you
as violence

red lanterns lighting
a greenish dusk

an empire of night
outreaching

you do not believe
in dying

your heart will spread
from its hollow walls

an emptiness
taking in anything

I'm beginning to see
where there is to get to

a kind of immortal
openness

to meet you in
the midst of your darkness

this is the message
you've been tapping out

in your silent
perseverance

be wiser thou
          go in go
in if you cannot see through

go in to the shelter
of ongoingness

The Book of Retreat

2012

In the years to come, we will know it as
the book of retreat. Concerned for the most
with winter fuel, gathering sticks
in the falling wood, with how to live
well, productive, covered in mud
and coal dust, ash, spitting the bitterness
out as it rose, learning to see
usefulness differently. At the end of the track,
camps built up around churches, capitols
burnt, nations marched on themselves,
crying for evolution, very
softly, armed with bombs and libraries.
Each night on the tv news, we watched
prophets in suits debating the shape
of the end. While we sat, apostatic,
wet-eyed, feeling the miles extend
between us and them as though broken and stretched.
We were very far and poor in hours
and travel expenses, and most of all,
rich in each other, growing old
and fat on the thin brown soup of the land.
In the years to come, when everything's happened,
we'll see the pattern. We'll know it as vision.
We'll say *we knew all along.*

Disability Rebellion/Plague Year Season 6

Lie down lie down on the grass on the growing
in the lyrical ditch of the present moment
in the trench of it. Let this be our protest –
our bodies corresponding to the earth – a rogue
equilibrium. Eyes never so open. Limbs
sinking into revelation. In a wood,
in a field, on a lawn, by a wall, in the road,
in the sticky centre of a supermarket aisle,
on the cold tiles of parliament, on a pocket of time
mown short. Lie down. What you feel is a forced
evolution of terror. Find power in surrender.
Lie down and let yourself rise as you fall.
Repeat until you mean it. *The conditions*
of my body are incurable as entropy. The conditions
of society are not. Can you see it as you lie
on the ground you found for yourself? The something
of strangeness flickering in the distance? The promise
of belonging to a more splendid world?

Notes & Acknowledgements

With thanks as always to everyone who has supported me along the way: I hope you know who you are and how important you are to me. Thanks to everyone at Seren who brought this book into being. Especial thanks to Annie Rutherford and Emily Hasler for manuscript advice (and much more). Many of these poems are in conversation with other poems, writers and artists living and dead, and would be impossible without them.

'Not Dying' is published in *After Sylvia* (Nine Arches, 2022). 'Dislocation' came out of the same project and responds to the notion in Plath's poem 'Tulips' of a country as far away as health. A version of 'Letter in October' was published in *Magma* 86 (2023). 'The grey wagtail teaches' was included in Annie Rutherford's Poetry Advent Calendar, 2025. 'Frog Song', 'Fox/ Plague Year Season 3' and 'Pain Parade' were published in *Aftershock Review* Issue 1 (2025). 'Pain Parade' was written after an online workshop with Kirstie Millar for the CHASE Medical Humanities Network in 2023. All the characters in the poem can be seen parading through Leonora Carrington's 1952 painting 'Ulu's Pants' as well as through my body. 'Silver Birch', 'Sessile Oak', 'Larch' and 'Yew' form part of 'Five Lakeland Trees' in *Romantic Trees: The Literary Arboretum, 1740-1840* (Liverpool University Press, 2026). 'Yew' quotes from William Wordsworth's 'Lines Left Upon a Seat in a Yew-Tree…' and 'Yew-Trees'. 'Resolving' draws on New Year resolutions Virginia Woolf made on 2 January 1931: 'To have none. Not to be tied. To be free & kindly with myself […]'. 'The Limits of Music as Time Travel' was commended in the Ver Poets Prize 2022. A version of 'Petroglyph Way' was published in *Dark Mountain* (2018). 'A Message' was written in December 2023 and included in Annie Rutherford's Poetry Advent Calendar, 2024. It remixes lyrics from various Christmas carols, including 'O Little Town of Bethlehem', and 'O Holy Night'.

'As I lay down on the grass, I observed' was written for *Que(e)ry Points*, a collaborative project in English and German responding to the lives and writings of Dorothy Wordsworth and Annette von Droste-Hülshoff, co-created with Annie Rutherford and Anneke Lubkowitz and funded through Creative Scotland's Four Nations International Fund. 'As I lay down…' is also published in *Tendrils: Ecopoetics of Community and Justice* (Silver Press, 2026). It is in conversation with and quotes from the named writers, and the folk songs 'I wish, I wish' as sung by Marth Tilston, and 'Lord Randal' where it influences Edna St. Vincent Millay's poem 'Journey', as well as many translations of the German word 'taumel'.

A version of 'High Dam, Mid-September' is published in *Ten Poems From the Lake District* (Candlestick Press, 2025). 'Self Portrait as Didi' responds to artwork by Megan Fletcher responding to my book *Some of Us Just Fall* (Sceptre, 2023). 'Glow Up' was written after a guided meditation led by Maya Jordan at one of Vik Bennett's Wild Woman Writers' Salons. 'Sing the things you see' takes its title from the 'Lost Words Blessing' from the 2019 album *Spell Songs*, by Jim Molyneux, Beth Porter, Seckou Keita, Karine Polwart, Julie Fowlis and Rachel Newton, inspired by *The Lost Words* by Jackie Morris and Robert Macfarlane, a favourite of Jamie's. 'True Poetry' responds to an email sent to a Palestinian writer which declared a poetry event by a Palestinian poet in 2025 to be counter to 'true poetry', as quoted. 'Ottering' incorporates statistics about (effectively non-existent) Personal Independence Payment fraud rates. 'The Book of Retreat' was published in *Rialto* 76 (2012). 'Disability Rebellion/Plague Year Season 6' responds to a July 2025 die-in in Parliament, protesting against welfare cuts, during which disabled protestors were threatened with anti-terror legislation which had been used that month to proscribe anti-genocide activists. It quotes from Dorothy Wordsworth's *Grasmere Journal* from 29 April 1802.